A Funny Thing Happened at 27,000 Feet...

Craig Cormick is an award-winning Canberra-based journalist and author. He has published several anthologies of fiction with Mockingbird Press, including *The King of Patagonia* (1999), *The Queen of Aegea* (2001) *and the Princess of Cups* (2003), which was shortlisted for the Queensland Premier's Steele Rudd Award.

A Funny Thing Happened at 27,000 Feet...

Tales from Times of Terror
by Craig Cormick

Mockingbird
An imprint of
GINNINDERRA PRESS

'Stuffed' was previously published in *Silverfish New Writing 5*, Malaysia, 2005
and in *Chrome #2*, Malaysia, 2005.

A Funny Thing Happened At 20,000 Feet: Tales From Times of Terror
ISBN 978 1 74027 337 4
Copyright © Craig Cormick 2005

First published 2005
Reprinted 2016

GINNINDERRA PRESS
PO Box 3461 Port Adelaide 5015
www.ginninderrapress.com.au

Contents

'The only thing we have to fear is fear itself.'

– Franklin D. Roosevelt

'I only have two fears in this world: one being nuclear war…the other? Carnies…smmaalll hands…smell like cabbage.'

– Austin Powers

A Funny Thing Happened
at 27,000 Feet...

I dislike flying at the best of times, but waking up four hours into an eight-hour flight and seeing Osama Bin Laden standing there in the aisle, waving a Coke bottle around and threatening everyone in garbled Arabic or something – that really sucks!

My first thought was that this was some kind of alcohol- and fever-induced bad dream. I'd picked up some virus in Africa and had been sitting at the airport in Johannesburg, having popped my last Panadol, feeling like shit, waiting for the flight back to Australia. All around me travellers had pulled their wheelie suitcases and belongings into little groups, like forming wagon-train circles against all the touts and sleazebags and shady characters wondering around the terminal, I guess.

That's when I saw him for the first time, and I thought, fuck, he looks just like Osama Bin Laden! Who'd choose to walk around an airport looking like that? He was probably a British citizen really, and sold cardboard boxes or something, but sitting there in the airport terminal like that, you'd swear it really was Osama Bin Laden. White robes and headgear and all.

He sat on one of the aluminium chairs at the far end of the lounge, with some people staring at him and some ignoring him, both the filthy rich and the plain filthy. But what did I care if he wanted to dress like Bin Laden? I felt like shit and I just wanted to get onto the plane home and close my eyes. I missed the carpeted luxury of even the rattiest Australian economy airport terminal. I'd had my share of Africa and just wanted to go home.

When the shuttle bus finally arrived to take us out to the plane, I saw him again, standing there in his robes. He was taller than I'd imagined him to be. If it was him, of course, which I didn't really think it was. Why would the real Osama Bin Laden be dumb-arse enough to walk around an airport dressed like himself? He'd shave his beard off, or wear a hat that covered his face more or put on a Groucho Marx disguise or something. Even dressing as Salman Rushdie would be safer than dressing like that.

Or maybe this guy just did it for the attention. I remember when I saw Elton John at an airport once and slowly worked up the nerve to ask him for his autograph. He wrote *Oiva Vuotulainen*. It turned out he was a Finnish opera singer, but he loved the way people mistook him for Elton John.

When the Osama look-alike got to the front of the security queue, I saw the African guys there shared some joke with him and they all laughed. And that made me think of that bit in the film *Michael Collins*, when all the British police in Ireland are searching for him, and he's stopped at a checkpoint, and they ask, 'Name?' and he says, 'Michael Collins!' And they all burst out laughing.

I mean, you could imagine it happening. If Osama Bin Laden was going to sneak onto a plane anywhere in the world, dressed as himself, Johannesburg would be the place.

*****

A funny thing had happened in Cape Town a couple of days earlier. I was walking back to my hotel from the harbour front one evening, and I was just starting to feel the first effects of the fever. I'd been trying to get a ride across to Roben Island but there were no seats on the ferry. It had all been booked out by local schoolkids and African tourists. I felt really cranky about that. Like I wanted to shout that I'd come halfway around the world to visit Roben Island, and it wasn't fair that all these kids who were locals were getting to go instead. But I had this deep down unreasonable fear that the school kids might stick a tyre on my neck and light it if I did. Or maybe I'd just spent too much time wandering around the Apartheid Museum looking at photos of the bad old days, and it had me spooked.

Everything wasn't so black and white any more.

It was almost dark as I was walking back to the hotel, and everybody everywhere had been warning me to watch out for muggers. But after the first few days I began to relax a little. I stopped crossing the street every time I saw somebody approaching me. Stopped averting my eyes every time an African walked past me. I felt I had earned some right to walk along the streets with a jaunt to my step. Felt I had earned some right to temporary invulnerability.

Well, there I was just walking down the street, one block away from the hotel and this African guy stops me and asks if I have any change for food. I look him over and he's polite and looks down at the ground, like he really does just need money for food, so I take out a few rand and give them to him.

'Thank you, sir. Thank you, sir,' he says to me and walks off.

And you know, I felt really good about that. Like I'd somehow done something significant to combat third world debt. Like I was as important as Bono when it came to combating poverty.

And then suddenly there was another young African in front of me. Standing just like the first. Hand out low, eyes down. 'Please sir. Please. Can you give me some money for food?'

And I say, perhaps too quickly, 'Sure.' And I reach into my pocket for a few more rand. I fumble with the notes and give him some, and he looks at the money and then looks at me.

He holds my gaze and says, 'This is not enough!'

I reach into my pocket, a little surprised at his boldness, and give him a few more rand.

He looks at it and I'm waiting for him to show some gratitude when he says, 'And your watch! Give me that too!' His eyes are locked on mine, and there's this menace in his voice now, making me feel ill at ease.

I hesitate a moment, trying to think of something to say, but I take my watch off and give it to him, and he puts it on.

'And your camera,' he says.

'I don't have my camera with me,' I lie.

He pulls a face. Disappointed in me. 'Then your shoes,' he says.

'My shoes?'

'Yes!'

I take them off too. Watch him try them on.

Then it is my hat. My belt. My sunglasses. He lets me keep all the cards in my wallet, though. He says they are useless. I feel a strange urge to tell him that the credit cards can be useful for scraping ice off your windscreen in winter, but keep my mouth shut.

Then he's done. And he says, 'Thank you. Thank you, sir.' And he walks off. That jaunty African gait to his steps.

And I go back to the hotel wondering if I'd been mugged or had just been persuaded to give my things away.

***

So there I am, at twenty-something thousand feet, waking up from a troubled sleep, with a fevered headache, and I see this Osama Bin Laden look-alike standing there in front of me, waving a bottle of Coca-Cola in a menacing fashion. It must be a bad dream, I think. But I'd just woken from a dream, albeit a dream of Halle Berry in her Catwoman outfit. And although it was a bad movie it was a pretty good dream. So I'm rubbing my eyes and thinking, if that was the dream, then this must be…what? Real? Surreal?

I look around the plane and I can see that everyone is staring at this guy. Just staring at him. Like they're thinking, no way this is the real Osama Bin Laden. No way!

'Fucksake,' I mumble. And then he steps right in front of me. He's screaming at everybody in Arabic or something. And the smell of petrol hits me hard in the nostrils. He's hijacking us with a petrol bomb in a Coke bottle!

He says something again, which might have been in Arabic, or might have been in English, but his accent is really appalling. No wonder he gets people to subtitle the videos he sends out. He tries shouting louder at us, that old ploy of American tourists when you're confronted by somebody who doesn't speak English, but it's apparent that still nobody understands him. He turns around and screams something and some underling comes running up to us from the back of the plane, and I turn my head and see that there are at least two more hijackers back there, also waving bottles of Coke around at the passengers. Osama, or the Osama-wannabe, presses a small cassette into his lackey's fingers and he turns and runs back down to the rear of the plane. Then *Everybody Loves Raymond* cuts out on the onboard monitors, they flicker a bit, and there's this tape of Osama playing and he's still ranting in Arabic, but the tape is subtitled in blurry English.

And I see this instant look of shock on the faces of all the people about me. It *is* Osama Bin Laden! They look at the monitor, and then look at him, and then back at the monitor. Like seeing it on TV makes it real.

The subtitle words on the video are things like 'The World will know the meaning of peril. The Almighty wills it that his warriors will mow down there enemiees like chaff before the hoarse.'

Chaff before the hoarse? How can anybody expect to terrorise people with bad spelling, I wonder.

Then he starts ranting in the aisle again, but he could have been talking about the perils of deep vein thrombosis for all I know.

But then the lackey is back and screams at everyone, 'Nobodee move or you will all dieeee!'

And of course that sets a wave of terror running through the cabin. I can smell the petrol heavily when he waves it about and I think for a moment that I'm going to throw up on Bin Laden. I try and hold it in. To quote Shania Twain, I don't think it would impress him much.

***

At the airport, going through security, they'd made me take off my belt and then my shoes, just like the guy in Cape Town had, and I'd gone back and forward through the metal detector, over and over, holding up my pants with one hand, feeling embarrassed as the crowd backed up further and further behind me. They took it with good humour, though; after all, it wasn't them slowly stripping for the security guys. And the lady in front of me had her tweezers and nail clippers confiscated. Does somebody really think it might be possible to hijack a plane with a pair or tweezers? 'Nobody move or I'll pluck the air hostess's eyebrows!' Or maybe the airlines were planning to melt them all down and build new parts with them to offset the high cost of petrol of something?

And that made me think, all that money spent on airport security, and how much did Bin Laden's one-litre Coke bottle of petrol cost? Not even two dollars. Less if he had any of those supermarket petrol discount vouchers!

***

So there we are at twenty-something thousand feet, feeling the full emptiness of it beneath us. Our seatbelts and safety devices are now our shackles. The plane feels like it's vibrating more than normal, although maybe I can just feel it more. It fills my whole body. And I remember reading that in the early days of planes, before they got more clever at building them, nuts and bolts and bits would regularly shake loose, which makes me wonder what the vibrations might be doing to us when we fly.

When the plane banks left or right, I can feel it through my whole body. The pull of the aircraft. Like we're joined together somehow.

Bin Laden's English is starting to become a little clearer. He's made a joke, I think, telling us that when a plane flies to the east the day is shorter, and this day might be very short. But nobody laughs. Maybe they still can't understand him. If we did laugh, maybe it would appease him. Then I have this sudden fever-induced great insight. That's his problem, he's a frustrated stand-up comedian!

Now he's explaining to us what will happen when he explodes the petrol bomb. Something about how it will burn out the in-flight systems and cause us to crash. He's telling us that he's an engineer and that he knows these things. Like he knew just how to bring down the twin towers of the World Trade Centre. He seems very proud of that.

And then he waits, far too long really, and tells us that that one really brought down the house. No one laughs.

He's better live than he is on TV, you know, but I'll bet none of his lackeys have ever had the nerve to tell him that his delivery timing sucks.

***

On the last day in Africa I took a tour down to the Cape of Good Hope. The 'most south-western' part of the African continent, we were told. Not the most southern, that was further around to the east.

Our driver was an affable white guy in his late forties or early fifties. He was a bit of an amateur comedian too. Driving out of the suburbs of Cape Town he started telling us about his years in the South African army spent in Angola. 'It was a real blast,' he says, and turns around to see if anybody laughs. Nobody does. He frowns and tells us that he spent eight years crawling around in the bush shooting at the blacks. And then, suddenly it all changed. And now he pays a black man to crawl around his bushes and shoot at white burglars. Still no laugh.

So he does the serious part of the routine. His world fell apart with democracy, you know. A lot of his ex-army buddies couldn't take it and fled to Perth or the UK or other places they could continue to be unreconstructed racists. But he stayed behind. It was his country too, he said. And he felt it would be betraying something to run away. Now he has our attention.

'And now,' he says, 'ten years after true democracy, I'm very proud to be a South African. I'm proud to have had Nelson Mandela as my president. He's a truly great man.'

We all nod solemnly, with a reverence reserved for people like Mandela, the Dalai Lama and Ian Thorpe. And then he says, 'It's lucky I'm a bad shot or we might not have had him for our president, eh?'

***

Bin Laden is ranting again about injustice, asking us all these questions I'm not sure if he really wants us to answer or not. Like what do we think is the main cause of the moral corruption of the West? And what do we think they are fighting for?

I look around to see if anybody on the plane wants to venture a guess. And I see, down the front from me, there's a Wesley Snipes look-alike. Way to go! If anybody's going to lean over and punch out Osama's lights, it's going to be him. But he just sits there.

Then one of his lackeys starts leading people up to the toilets, in pairs. About time too. Osama has everybody so shit-scared that we're all busting to go. And I remember reading that during the Moscow theatre siege they made everybody shit in the orchestra pit. Or was that only because somebody escaped out of the toilet window? No one would be trying that on this plane, though.

I look around the plane a bit more and see there's a Bruce Willis look-alike up behind me. That's good, I think. He'll have experience in dealing with terrorists. Though I then recall that in *Die Hard 2* he actually blew up the plane to stop the baddies.

And then, despite not really wanting to, I'm remembering all the terror plane movies I've ever seen. Even this one about killer bees that were genetically modified and escaped on a plane and were stinging people and blood was pouring out their eyes and everybody was running around screaming and dying. Death seems more real when you see the blood, of course.

***

So our Afrikaans tour guide, Jan the bus driver, is telling us to keep our eyes open as we drive into the parking lot at the Cape. 'Look sharp,' he says. 'Over there! Over there!' And he points at a man walking back from the café with a milk shake in each hand.

And as we watch, one of the many baboons around the car park jumps off the roof of a car and goes into a stalk pose, running quickly at the man and then it pounces on him. It knocks the man to the ground, grabs the milkshakes and heads off into the bush, spilling all the contents of course.

The tourist, who sounds American, is screaming for help, grabbing to see if he's still got his wallet and camera, not really understanding what has just happened. Probably thinking he's just been mugged.

Jan is doubled up laughing so hard he has to stop the bus. 'He's lucky the baboon didn't bite him,' he says. Then, 'I love this job.'

***

So I'm sitting there on the plane reading the in-flight magazine to take my mind off things and there's this article about the top ten ways there are to die. Heart disease, stroke, falling down, cancer, suffocation, drowning, car crashes, diabetes, pneumonia, Alzheimer's. And the point of the article is that the main causes of death are all lifestyle-related diseases. So I take out my pen and start writing in the margin: bullets, starvation, machete cuts, knife wounds, petrol bombs and plane crashes.

And then I'm thinking about the Lockerby plane bombing. Thinking of all those bodies in seats falling to the earth. What it must have felt like, falling through space, strapped into your chair, clutching the arm rests frantically like your life depended upon it, when really it wouldn't make the slightest difference. What must the terror of that feel like, staring down at the ground below the clouds, falling into your own grave? Would it be a moment of fulfilling revelation to be plummeting back to earth, or would it be so terrifying that you'd wish you died in a single fiery explosion? How much terror could you take? And what would be left? Body parts, the detritus of passports and shoes and handbags and plane pillows and meals. How long would it take to reassemble the jigsaw puzzle of the plane and the people aboard it, to ensure that all the gathered pieces of the person were in the right plastic body bags?

Whose body parts might I share a grave with? I wonder. The foot of that fat man in front of me? The arm of the old lady across the aisle? A piece of breast from the young woman two seats down and across? Just a piece perhaps.

All they'd find of us if Bin Laden sets off his petrol bomb when we're over land would be a large and ugly scar of metal and debris ploughed into the ground. Suitcases and bags and papers and clothing. And bits of bodies. Or would we be incinerated in a mighty fireball and fall back to earth as soft ashen rain?

Why does my brain keep thinking of these things? I wonder. Perhaps it's the fever. Why can't I think of the Halle Berry Catwoman dream again?

And then, despite myself, I'm thinking of the guy who hijacked the plane between Melbourne and Tasmania using two wooden sticks. And there was that other nutter who had the bomb in his shoe. I note that no one ever used tweezers or nail clippers, though! That's the secret to success at things, I conclude. Your imagination is a bigger weapon than a gun. Just ask Osama Bin Laden there with his petrol bomb.

***

We'd climbed to the top of the cliff overlooking the Cape of Good Hope and had taken dozens of photographs, while Jan stayed in the car park to see a small boy get abducted by baboons and a lady have her purse snatched. Young African boys with whips were searching the nearby shrubbery for them when we got back.

'Ah you should have seen it,' said Jan excitedly.

'We saw a whale!' we tell him. 'We could clearly see it out there in the ocean, the waves breaking around its back, facing out towards the whole southern ocean. It was fantastic.'

'Jaaa,' Jan said, 'that's not actually a whale. It's the most photographed rock in South Africa.' And he started laughing again.

We looked at each other and frowned. We'd taken dozens of shots of it. And I could see the others were thinking exactly the same thing as me. Would we still tell people it was a rock when we showed them our photos?

And I wonder if I should I tell this to Bin Laden now. If all the passengers tell him about all the photos they've taken that they are planning to show their children and parents and friends and colleagues, would that make any difference? We must have thousands of pictures there on the plane, as prints, or on discs and memory cards.

Or would he just say that we should take out our cameras and snap our last pictures of each other so that our children and parents and friends and colleagues would know something of our last moments when they recovered the wreckage of the plane? He might even let us take a photo with him, with one of us holding two fingers up behind his head. That'd give us the last laugh, eh?

***

I spent several hours at the local craft markets in Cape Town, wandering around the stalls, talking to the owners and bargaining for items. The routine was pretty much always the same. 'My friend, my friend, my friend. You are my lucky customer for today. You must buy something from me to bring me luck. I will give you a special price.'

But there is one man, selling wooden masks, who doesn't have the same routine. He looks desperate and a little angry, and I can see he's not going to pretend that I'm any friend to him.

'You buy a mask?' he asks me.

I nod a little and look at them. 'Where is this one from?' I ask, pointing to an ornate black wooden one.

'This is from the Ivory Coast,' he says. 'Far from here.'

He has a slight French accent, and so I ask him, 'Is that your home?'

'No,' he says. 'I come from Rwanda. You have heard about the troubles there, yes?'

And it seems very important to him that I know something about Rwanda, so I say, 'Yes. Of course. Terrible troubles.'

He nods. Somewhat satisfied. And then I want to show him that I'm not just bullshitting him, but I do know something of Rwanda, and I wonder if I should ask him whether he's a Hutu or a Tutsi. But I can't remember what the difference is. Which group were responsible for the massacres? And weren't they in their own turn massacred? I wonder if it will insult him more to ask or not to ask.

So I point at my toes and say, 'In Australia, these are tootsies.' I look at his face and it's more a mask than any of the wooden carvings that he's selling.

***

Osama is trying another joke out now, but he still can't get the accent clear enough to be understood by everyone. Something about the haves and have nots and have yachts.

And I've decided he's not going to blow us up until we're at least over somewhere important. Why would he waste a good aeroplane when he could crash it into something, even if there's not much worth crashing into in Perth. Maybe he'll make us fly all the way to Sydney. There's plenty of targets there. The Opera House. The Sydney Harbour Bridge. Or maybe he thinks he'll find a target in Canberra? He'll regret that, circling the city over and over looking for something worthwhile to crash into.

And that makes me think of Mohammad Attas, the leader of the 11 September hijackers. That one with the spooky dark eyes. Did he rant at all the passengers like Bin Laden is doing? Tell them lame-arse Egyptian jokes? Like why did the Israeli cross the road? Or did he determine to convert them to understanding his vision through silence? Let the passengers know he was ready to die by not saying anything at all?

Or perhaps he told them that they could still be saved and then, as he turned towards the towers, giving them the punch line, that it would only happen by embracing Allah in the last seconds of their lives.

I look up and see the in-flight monitors say that it is minus 60 degrees Centigrade outside and our air speed is 550 kilometres per hour.

And then I think of a punchline that Jan the bus driver had told me. He'd been saying that Australia and South Africa weren't that different really, it was just circumstances of fate that had taken them on their different paths. And I could as well have been born him, or any other person in the world, rich or poor, but you had to just do the best with the life you had. You could travel all over the globe and see both wonders and injustice, and it made you think about your place in things, but it was what you took back to your own day-to-day life that mattered, for you had to find your own philosophy for living. And then he'd pointed out the window to where some swamp birds were standing and said, 'Remember those birds when you leave Africa.'

'How do you mean?' I asked.

'Leave all your egrets behind, eh?'

***

I can see the passengers about me are all tired and frightened. Most are looking into their laps, or holding hands with the person beside them. I wish I had somebody beside me to hold, but I've an empty seat. It could be worse, though. I could have that big fat hairy guy from three rows down beside me.

Now Bin Laden is going on about something to do with a pan-Islamic nation stretching from Africa through to Asia. His English is too crappy to fully understand. Something about the oppressed of the world's raisin cup. Or maybe he meant 'rising up?' Who knows?

And then the Wesley Snipes guy goes into action. He puts his hand up and, when Osama turns to him, he says he can't understand what the hell he's saying. Osama blinks at him, like he's just been heckled. I look to the Bruce Willis look-alike, to see what he'll do. But he doesn't look so much like Bruce Willis any more. He looks more like he might be some poor English cardboard box salesperson wishing he'd taken a different flight.

Then a stewardess stands up, and she does bear some resemblance to Jennifer Garner, and she says he will need to talk a little clearer if he wants us to understand him.

Osama blinks again, at her, and then he screams for his lackey, who has been escorting people to the toilet. You can see he's bored by it and resents being the toilet monitor. The lackey comes running down and grabs the stewardess by the arms and Osama pulls out a ring pull he's snapped off an in-flight drink tin, and he cuts her about the face. She screams and drops to her knees. I don't think she's hurt real bad, but there's a lot of blood. And death seems more real when you see blood, right.

And then Osama stands back and says something and holds his hands out, as if he's just performed some trick. Waiting for somebody to applaud him. But nobody does.

A little old lady about three seats in front of me starts it. She goes, 'Boooh!' and holds her hands up to her mouth to make it louder.

Then another lady is doing it too. Then some of the men. All booing as loud as they can.

And that's when I do it. I take out my own drink bottle, which is still mostly full, and I throw it at Bin Laden. It hits him right on the head and he stumbles back a little bit, shocked by it. Enraged by it.

'No egrets,' I mumble.

It's obvious that none of his lackeys have ever dared boo him or throw things at him when he's practising his routines.

And then there's a sudden avalanche of tins and bottles and books and shoes all being pelted at him. He goes down under the onslaught. And people about me are shouting, in anger and rage and fury and others are laughing hysterically.

And suddenly it's the lackey who looks terrified. He stands there, fumbling with his matches, trying to light his fire bomb, saying, 'Enough. No more laughing now!'

Day Cruise

'The old Frenchman will be the first one to go,' I whisper to Angelique. 'I'll take money on it.' I mean, you could just see it in his face. The way he kept looking to the ship's railing. Or perhaps he was looking to the horizon, hoping it would help to stop his head rocking. But the horizon always seemed to be moving too.

That was a good line, I thought. I could use that. Some metaphor about no matter how calm things seem, the horizon is always moving. Maybe.

'I hope he spews on top of the Americans,' she whispers back. 'God, that American couple can talk.'

Although I don't think either would notice if the old French guy did throw up on them. They're actually a mother and daughter – the Americans. They're also a twin stand-up act after a few rums. They're sitting there now on the far side of the table, laughing and telling the rest of us about their last holiday in Bermuda.

'But so expensive,' they say. 'More than you'd think.'

'And then that thing happened,' the daughter says. She's like, maybe eighteen, and her mother, who is like, maybe forty-four, ignores her and keeps talking.

The British couple nod and tut-tut; although they've never actually been to Bermuda themselves, they agree that prices these days are 'just terrible'.

Kenyan prices were just terrible and Algeria was just terrible. And Egypt – well – the prices in Egypt were just terrible.

There are ten of us on this boat, though they promote it as a yacht. A pair of Brits, French, Americans, Canadians and me and Angelique. It is hard to know how many crew there are, as there is always another new face wondering up from down below. They are all dark-skinned, dark-eyed, strong and silent. Quietly Islamic, I might describe them as.

There are two women in the galley, cooking our lunch, who we only catch glimpses of as the galley door opens and closes. There's another good metaphor in there, I think. Something about the hidden world of Islamic women. I'd like to ask them what they think of being crew on this yacht full of rich Westerners, who drink alcohol and wear skimpy clothes, and complain about prices everywhere and in their country in general.

The guy who brings us our food from the galley is completely silent. He just stares at us all like he knows something that we don't. He particularly stares at the American ladies. Like he hasn't seen an American for a long, long time. Maybe he hasn't. Momma and daughter tell us how difficult it is to find somewhere to travel to that they consider 'safe' any more. Now they're complaining again about how much some knick-knack cost them in the local markets. This in front of a crew who make about $10 a day, working six days a week.

And then the Brits and Americans start counting off on their fingers all the places that are no longer safe to travel to. East Africa. Egypt. Israel. Thailand. India. Algeria. Sri Lanka. Central America. Columbia. Venezuela.

'Bermuda,' says the American daughter.

Her mother nods and keeps going. 'Northern Ireland. Indonesia. Any former Soviet Republic. Turkey. The Maldives.'

I'm impressed. They really know their geography. Yet, I notice that neither of them says London. But you can see it in the American's eyes. See the way she wants to say it, but doesn't want to isolate her new compatriots. Fellow world travellers. Fellow targets.

The Canadian couple watch this bemusedly, in the knowledge that nobody hates Canadians, and the French couple shrug with disinterest, in the knowledge that everybody hates the French.

Then there's a pause, like they're considering just what a dangerous place the world has become. Like they're wondering just how safe they might be even here.

'Are you thinking what I think you're thinking?' whispers Angel.

'Yes. I'm thinking I could use this,' I say.

'It's good,' she says.

We sit at the little side table across from the other four couples and talk softly. We've gotten good at this over time, talking about people around us without them knowing it. It's all in the eyes, really, not staring at the people you're talking about. Not giving it away.

We'd planned to learn Esperanto once, as absolutely nobody would ever catch us talking about them in Esperanto. But, you know how it is, it never caught on. So we just got very good at whispering in each other's ears, pretending we were mumbling romantic sweet nothings.

'Consider this,' I say. 'What if the crew are fanatics?'

She smiles.

'And today's the day, right?'

She nods.

'That ever-present tension from the Islamic crew. What if they've reached the point of snapping? Today they throw in their $10 a day and become martyrs for Allah. Seven virgins in heaven, or however many it is, are waiting for them. And each of them more attractive than any of the middle-aged Westerners they escort on these cruises around the islands.'

She nods again.

'It wouldn't take much. They've pretty well got us prisoner here. They could drug our food. They could just pull out a couple of guns. Hell, a few steak knives would probably be enough.'

Angel smiles. She likes it.

That's something to work on, I think. Looking into the dark silent face of the waiter. The unstated but ever-present fear that the crew are hostile. That'd work.

'It's going to be a stage play,' I say. 'The set made up like a yacht.'

'Ten of us plus the crew is a big cast,' says Angel. 'You'll need to get rid of someone.'

'Hmmm,' I say into her ear. 'I'll have to keep the Americans. And the French make a good contrast with each other.'

He's about seventy, I reckon – that Frenchman. A little frail with white hair, and you can just tell it wasn't his idea to come out on an island cruise for the day. You can see how seasick he's been since we left the dock. His wife is probably about twenty years or so his junior. Maybe she'd been a second or a third wife, about twenty years ago. I could build on that. She's a real sun-worshipper, but has had too much of it. She has skin like leather. She rolls up her sarong and rolls down her bikini top whenever she goes out on the deck, to get the maximum amount of sun. It's like having a tan in a designer label.

That's another good line, I think.

The British are probably in their sixties. They seem to have travelled absolutely everywhere. Except Bermuda, of course. But they seemed bored by it all. As if the novelty of travel has long since worn off. Yet they have some need to keep travelling. Like it's just what they do. Less boring than not travelling. They don't even take pictures, can you believe it?

'Maybe the Canadians,' I say.

They're young. Probably in their late twenties, but it could be more. Their unbridled enthusiasm makes them seem younger.

'But you'd lose the way that both the British and American couple keep trying to claim them as theirs,' says Angel.

'Then who?'

She thinks a moment. 'Why not start with a dead body? Shock the audience. Take control of their emotions.'

'How dead?' I ask.

'Really dead. Well, as dead as you expect any body to be in a play.'

'I like it. I like it a lot.'

She sticks her tongue in my ear. Just the tip of it. Makes me laugh. The others give us a quick glance and I have trouble keeping from looking up at them.

'Okay,' I whisper to Angel when the conversation at the other table has built up a head of steam again, 'I'm going to kill the American mother.'

'Too easy.'

'What's wrong with easy? Can't you imagine it? After she's had a few more rums?'

'But then what?' she asks.

'I was thinking of a bit of sexual tension,' I say.

'The daughter?'

'Who else?'

'With the French or the British?'

I roll my eyes at her. She smiles.

I say, 'She goes down below to the toilet, and coming back she steps into the passage and bumps into one of the crew. It's so dark she can't see his face. Only his eyes. She tries to squeeze past him, and he puts his hands out and touches her body. Or she thinks he does, but can't quite be certain. She emerges back into the dining area, flushed and giddy, aware that something has happened, but not sure what.'

'Hmmm,' says Angel. 'Would you show it in scene, or tell it in dialogue?'

'I'm undecided.'

I look up again at our fellow day-trippers, still drinking and talking. The American momma is asking if any of the others have seen the remake of Rodgers and Hammerstein's *South Pacific* with Glenn Close in it. 'It was fabulous,' she says. 'That's what settled it for me to take this holiday. Find a remote island somewhere. Maybe even a romantic encounter.'

Her daughter puts her finger in her mouth and mimes vomiting. 'Do any of you know the name of that French actor who played her lover?' she asks, turning to the French couple. 'You must know him. Very handsome. Long hair and a beard.'

But they don't know him. They say that they've not even seen the film. It was probably banned by some French anti-kitsch censorship board.

The conversation at the table then turns to different reality TV shows that everybody has seen that are set on tropical islands. It makes me think.

But Angel knows what I'm pondering and says, 'Stick to the story at hand. What happens next?'

'Okay,' I say, 'How about both the Americans are dead at the start?'

'But what about the sexual tension with the daughter?'

'Hmmm. Maybe I will use the Canadians.'

'I'm sure they wouldn't object.'

'So everybody is terrified, see. Not sure if they might be next or not.'

She nods a little.

'The French are in denial, of course. They keep saying it will be all right, as long as everyone obeys their captors.'

She nods again.

'But the Brits aren't convinced,' I whisper. 'They think they're going to be next. So they're working on the Canadians. Trying to get them to do something. Jump the guards or swim for help.'

'But they don't, of course.'

'Or maybe they do. But they get killed for it.'

'So the British couple have effectively killed them.'

'Yes.'

'It's good. The slow slip to the immoral from the moral.'

'Who is guilty and who is guiltless?'

'So how do they kill them?'

'A gun to the head is traditional.'

'Onstage or offstage?'

'Onstage has more impact.'

'But you couldn't do it again. How would you top it?'

I think about that.

'And what about the crew?' she asks. 'Do they go through a mirror process? Immoral back to moral?'

I think about that too. 'That's very good,' I say. 'No wonder you're my muse.'

She sticks the tip of her tongue into my ear again. I reach under the table and grope her under her skirt. Our faces show nothing.

'Watch this,' I whisper and I turn to the group at the table beside us and interrupt them with a slow and deep voice. 'Did any one notice on that last island we stopped to snorkel at, how much those small white shells on the beach looked like bones? Did any one else notice that?'

They all look at me and blink. The Frenchwoman pulls a face of great distaste.

'No?' I ask. She'll be next, I decide. The terrorists will kill her for pulling ugly faces just like that at them. Or just for being French. Angel would say it wouldn't work, but I'll find some way to kill Madame Leather-Skin off next. I smile at them all and turn back to Angel.

She can see what I'm thinking. 'Too many deaths and you've got a Shakespeare play,' she says.

'What about a rescue?'

'An implausible rescue and you've got a Bruce Willis screenplay.'

'So I'll leave it up in the air. Change the moral stances and question the audience's preconceived values of good and evil.

'Think it'll float?'

'Ha ha.'

'So why do they do it? The crew. What's their motive?'

'They're Islamic extremists.'

'They still need a motive.'

'Ransom some colleagues out of prison. Bali bombers perhaps.'

'Perhaps,' she says.

'And they come to understand that feeling of power,' I say. 'Of holding somebody's life in their hands.'

'Like an author,' she says.

'Behave or I'll put you in the play,' I say.

'So how does it all end? Who will save us?'

'I'm not sure yet.'

'It should come from within the cast you've already established.'

I nod. It will have to feel real. It will be a play about moral issues. And killing token Americans. That's how it would happen in real life. I look across to group at the table opposite. They are now talking about that wonderful unspoiled holiday location that everybody's heard whispers of, but nobody knows quite where it is.

'Even Antarctica is spoiled by tourists these days,' says the British woman.

I've heard this conversation too many times before so I kiss Angel and say, 'A bit of fresh air is needed.'

'Passive voice,' she chides as I stand up.

I step past our fellow tour party with a polite nod and wander out onto the deck to let my characters develop a bit more. Several of the crew are seated at the rear – the stern – watching the ship and the horizon, like we're just a temporary distraction from what's important in life. They talk quietly, looking out over the ocean, and I can see that they are smiling. Really smiling. Not stern at all, I think. They should call it something else. And I wonder if this how their ancestors had smiled, sailing these seas, and making it their world. No charts. Only the stars at night and their knowledge of the seas and winds.

Their language sounds less harsh out here. Not like the angry growls and trills they make about us in the cabin. The words are now like the small waves that lilt against the yacht.

I'd like to talk to them. Find out what they think of us. But I wonder if the truth might be more disappointing than how I could create it in my imagination. I mean, take away the unknown and the cultural and racial paranoia, and what have you got left?

I wander towards the front of the ship. It's about sixty metres long, I guess. Two masts, though we travel with the engines on. I imagine asking Angel to stand with me on the prow there and throw out our arms and shout, 'I'm on top of the world!' But I can imagine that Americans and Canadians and French and British doing it too. Lining up like it's another tourist attraction.

One more circuit of the yacht and I go back into the cabin.

Angel has pulled her chair a little bit closer to the other table and, as if she has been waiting for me to return, asks the American daughter, 'So just what was the thing that happened in Bermuda?'

And everybody stops and turns to her. And then they turn and look at the young woman.

She looks to her mother, as if waiting for her to tell the story, but she's clearly not going to. She just takes another long drink and closes her eyes. 'Well,' says the daughter, 'We were out on this day cruise. Pretty much like this one. Snorkelling and visiting islands, you know. But the boat wasn't as big nor as nice as this one. Well we're way out from land and suddenly this big dark guy, one of the crew, pulls out a machete and holds it against one of the passengers' necks, and he's screaming and hollering so we can't hardly understand him. And the passengers are all screaming too, and this man with the machete at his neck has his hands together like in prayer and he's crying, see, and maybe this big guy is high on drugs, or maybe he'd done some sordid deal with this other guy that hadn't gone right, or maybe he was a terrorist, or just crazy, or who knows what, because we never found out.' And she looks at her mother again, who still has her eyes closed. 'Because momma just pulled out her hand gun and shot him three times in the head.'

We all blink. Turn to her mother. She looks up and smiles a little. Pats her purse reassuringly.

'And he just dropped to the deck dead,' says the daughter. 'And I mean he was like – really dead. And she pauses for her mother to cut in.

'And despite all that,' momma says, 'we didn't even get a refund on the cost of the day tour.'

The rest of us, to tell you the truth, are a little bit stunned. No one seems to know what to say. We're a shocked audience. Captive for the full details of the story. Totally in her control. Damn it!

I sit back down next to Angel and rub my chin for a few moments, while Momma says she's need another large drink before telling us all about it. And I whisper, 'I've got this new idea…'

Stuffed

We take off our blindfolds and see him standing there at the front of the bus.

He is wearing a traditional Islamic cap on his head and his eyes are shielded behind thick sunglasses. He is clearly in command. He smiles and says, 'I imagine you all are perhaps a little curious about where we have taken you?'

I look around at the other journalists seated around me. They are frowning and trying to get a glimpse out of the window. It has been hot and sticky on the bus and I can see that most are looking a little concerned. There are men out there with guns.

'My name is Mustafa,' the man at the front of the bus says and bows deeply before us. 'And, please, consider me your guide for today.' He smiles.

Nobody around me smiles back. We are all disoriented and uncomfortable. I suspect worse is yet to come. Then Mustafa steps back and indicates that we can all disembark. There is an orderly push as we all try and get off the bus at once, and then look around to try and get our bearings. We are surprised to see that we have been brought to the National Museum.

The oldest journalist amongst us, an aged BBC correspondent, says, 'I had a bad feeling about this. Never volunteer to go to an interview in a blindfold. I learned that in Beirut.'

'I didn't volunteer,' I add.

'I was kept prisoner by some god-damned fringe terrorist group for two weeks there,' he says.

'Do you think we'll see terrorists?' ask the young lady from *The Washington Post*. This is her first overseas posting since graduating from journalism college.

'I doubt it,' says the BBC correspondent. 'Not at the National Museum under a tour being conducted by the Malaysian Board of Tourism.'

'Well I'm curious,' says a middle-aged correspondent who works for some German radio station none of us have ever heard of.

'We're all curious,' I mumble. 'We're just not all convinced we're going to see anything worthwhile.'

Everyone at the Australian Broadcasting Corporation bureau office had been curious indeed. The invitation to the mystery press briefing had been hand-delivered by a senior official from the Ministry of Tourism, with a promise of something unparalleled. We'd tossed a coin in the office several times to see who would be the lucky person to get to go. I lost, and so here I was!

They say we're a pretty cynical lot at the best of times, us journalists, but after a few too many over-hyped government press briefings and announcements you get to suspect there is more PR and less of an actual news story in each major event you're bussed to. But at least being here meant I didn't have to cover the opening of the new sewage plant at the new capital, Putra Jaya.

Mustafa claps his hands to get our attention and says in a loud voice, 'We are going to show you something very, very exciting today. Something we think will position Malaysia at the cutting edge fore-front of the twenty-first century, in regard to tourism technology.'

We all smile politely as if we've not heard this type of spiel before. We may be cynical, but we know enough to smile until we've had the free lunch that has been promised to us after the briefing.

'Ever been to this museum?' the correspondent from Reuters asks me, leaning in close. He'd not have visited it himself, since there was no bar here. He was one of those from the old school of journalism, who did their best writing after half a bottle of Scotch rather than after a degree. They were becoming increasingly rare these days. An endangered species really. Most younger journalists hung out at gyms and juice bars.

'Yeah, once,' I tell him. 'About a year or two ago.'

'What's to see?'

I shrug. 'Nothing you wouldn't expect to see in any other museum.'

He nods and looks back to the bus, as if considering sneaking back and having a sleep there. Then he shrugs too, and falls in behind the line of us that start following Mustafa as he beckons us to follow him into the building.

'Please keep close together,' he says. 'We have taken certain security measures for your protection, and you should not get separated from the group under any circumstances.'

'Yeah, yeah, yeah,' mutters the Reuters correspondent, but I look across to the dozen or so armed soldiers around.

I'm pretty sure they never had military guards here before.

Mustafa stops at the main door and turns to us once more. 'Cameras will not be permitted to be used inside, but we will be releasing approved photographs to you after the event.'

I can see the intrigue is starting to bother a few of my colleagues and a Texan woman from *Newsweek* mutters, 'Cut the crap already and tell us what we're here to see.'

Mustafa doesn't hear her, or politely pretends not to, and he turns and strides into the building. We follow him dutifully, the armed guards regarding us coldly.

Mustafa leads us up the broad wooden stairs in pairs just like we are a school group.

The Reuters correspondent, who is carrying a few kilos more around his belly than is recommended for walking up staircases, asks, 'What's up the top here?'

And I say, 'It was all glass cases full of ratty-looking stuffed animals.'

'Stuffed animals! Great!' he says. 'I'll ring my editor and get him to hold the front pages of all the major newspapers for that!'

And I remember how sad all the animals had looked. Worn and aged. And there had been endless lines of school kids all standing dutifully in front of exhibits while their teacher or tour guide explained to them what they were seeing. I remember the best part of the museum had been all these mannequins dressed up to represent the different tribal groups and different national dresses. I wonder if they're still here?

Mustafa waits at the top of the staircase, where a curtain has been erected across the doorway, until we are all gathered there, and then he says, 'You are about to see something quite unrivalled in the evolution of the modern museum.'

We all smile. Still hanging out for that free lunch. And then he turns and pulls aside the curtain. There is a collective gasp from the journalists as we walk into the exhibition. The glass cases are just as I remember them, but they are full of people! Sitting on high stools or standing there, looking forlornly about them.

The first glass case has an overweight man and woman in it. Clearly Americans by the pictures of George W. Bush on their T-shirts. They both wear thick sunglasses and baseball caps and look very miserable.

The *Newsweek* lady walks up closer to the glass and waves at them, but they don't appear to notice her. 'Can they see us?' she asks Mustafa.

'Only if they lean very close against the glass,' he says. 'We've designed the lighting so they can't see us easily.'

'Aha,' she says and makes a note in her pad.

I turn my head to look around. There are one or two people in each of the glass cases. In some instances, there has been some effort made to create some sort of setting for them. Seats and a TV or something, but others are quite bare.

Mustafa says proudly, 'It's a brand new concept, you see. Where we once arrested foreigners and deported them for offending our laws, we now put them on display.'

'But…but…but…' gasps the correspondent for Reuters, old enough to think that human rights was more important than a good story. 'But it's inhumane!'

'Not at all,' croons Mustafa. 'They are fed and have clean quarters and are fulfilling a responsible role for society. What could be more satisfying?'

No one answers.

'Moving on,' he says, 'you will see we've tried to capture the full diversity of types.'

The next case I look into has what appears to be an English busker in it, with his guitar lying by his feet. I look closely at the label on the glass case; it says the young man was busking without a licence.

I walk onto the next case. There is an elderly German couple there, sitting on low plastic seats, holding each other's hands. The label says they had insulted Malaysia on postcards they'd written.

The next case has a single woman, in dirty singlet and high-cut shorts and sandals. She has her arms crossed and stares out towards us with anger and defiance on her face.

'What did she do?' the *Newsweek* correspondent asks.

'Oh, very serious,' says Mustafa. 'She refused to cover her head and shoulders when visiting a Mosque. Became very agitated about women's rights.' He smiles and shakes his head.

The *Newsweek* woman writes something else in her pad.

The next case has another overweight couple in it. I don't need to read the label to know this one. Australian tourists! He has saggy white shorts that show his bum crack when he turns around and a T-shirt that says, 'Shagging Machine'. She has a T-shirt that is so tight her boobs almost poke holes in it and her shirt reads, 'I'm with stupid'. I'm guessing that they had offended dress and fashion sense somewhere. Anywhere, really.

'Are there any questions?' Mustafa asks, seemingly very pleased with the way things are going.

'Yes,' I say, raising my hand. 'What happened to all the animals?'

'Ah,' says Mustafa. 'A very good question indeed. The truth is that we found it increasingly difficult to keep our animals, as members of environmental terrorist groups had made it a habit of breaking into the museum and stealing them!'

'Why?' I ask. 'To set them free?'

But he doesn't see the joke. 'Ah,' he says, 'Who can tell what is in the minds of these extremist sects? In one month alone, we lost our crocodile and our best tiger.'

'Tragic,' mutters the correspondent from the German radio station that nobody has ever heard of.

'It was a crime,' says Mustafa. He looks around us, to see if anybody wishes to contradict him. 'But then we captured some of the terrorists,' he announces gleefully. 'And while deciding how best to punish them, we came upon the idea for the museum.' And he strides across to the last glass case, which is shrouded in darkness, and turns on a light switch.

There are two men inside. One bends away from the sudden lights, shielding his eyes, but the other does not move.

The Reuters correspondent walks up closely and stares at the unmoving figure. 'My God,' he says. 'He's dead!'

'Stuffed, to be precise,' says Mustafa. 'Quite the latest thing in high-technology taxidermy. Nothing but the best.'

The other man in the case looks about himself nervously and then presses his face towards the glass to look out at us. He is dressed in ragged greens and has long unkempt hair with small leaves stuck in it.

'Now, down this end of the hall,' says Mustafa, 'there's something I think you'll really be delighted with.' And he leads the journalists away.

I'm about to follow when the man in the case waves at me.

'Hey,' he shouts. I can hear his voice clearly, although muffled, through the glass. 'Hey, psst. Buddy,' he says. He has a thick American accent. 'You gotta help me!'

I turn and look at him.

'You gotta get me outta here,' he says.

'Do I?' I mouth casually.

'Call the US embassy,' he shouts. 'They'll send somebody to free me. They'll send marines to storm the building.'

I lean towards the glass, wondering how to tell him that he's not exactly Private Jessica Lynch, when he appears to reconsider.

'Wait,' he says. 'They've probably got FBI and CIA files on me and would rather leave me here.'

'So who should I call?' I mouth back at him, so that the others won't hear me but he will get my meaning.

He thinks for a moment and then says, 'Call Greenpeace. They'll be able to do something.'

'Do what?' I mouth to him.

'I dunno. They can chain themselves to the gates downstairs or something,' he says.

Not that that would really be of much help to him, I think. And I doubt they'd be interested unless he was a little cuter and furrier. But he's not cute. Only furry. And most of that seems to be algal growth on his skin.

'You gotta call someone,' he says, and snarls fiercely out at me. 'Come on, man, you gotta help me.'

I tilt my head to let him know that I am considering it, but I'm also remembering a story the Reuters correspondent had told me one night over drinks, about an animal liberation group who had released thousands of turkeys from some turkey farm in the USA a week before Thanksgiving. Most of the freed turkeys had all run onto a nearby highway and been killed by cars and trucks, causing several serious accidents, and most of the others had frozen to death.

Yet he looks so pathetic in that cage. Worse than the sad-looking stuffed tigers and bears had looked. I nod and point to him and then mime writing to let him know that I will write up his story. I will tell the world what has happened to him. After all, one person's eco-terrorist is another's eco-freedom fighter, right?

'Ah, there you are,' says Mustafa, putting an arm around me and turning me back towards the pack. 'I thought I'd lost somebody.'

'Tell me,' I say, in my most professional voice. 'What do you intend to do with the – ah – exhibits here? What will happen to them?'

'Well, in the interests of humanity we will eventually release these creatures back into their own environment. It is most touching to see them scuttle off into the international airport, you know.'

'And this one in particular?' I ask, pointing back to the greenie.

'Ah well,' he says, 'that's a bit more complex. His natural habitat is slowly being eroded by progress and he might have to stay with us for a very very long time.'

'Oh,' I say. 'I'm asking because I was thinking of writing a story about him and his colleague. I think it would make very interesting reading.'

'Yes. Yes, I'm sure it would,' says Mustafa. 'But I'd be very careful what I write if I were you.'

'Why's that?'

But he doesn't say. He just leads me over to the glass exhibit case where he has left the rest of the party. They are staring silently at the lone forlorn figure inside it, and at the sign, which reads 'Hostile journalist. Dangerous. Do not feed.'

American Dream

Madam Sylvia tells me that I don't sleep well. She barely glances at my palm as she says it, looking more at the crowd walking past on the sidewalk. She says I will live a long time. Says the one I love is far away. Says I want love, but will always be unlucky in love.

Her little shop spills out across the sidewalk of the historic quarter of Philadelphia. She's sitting on an iron garden chair, like somebody's grandmother, sipping on a cool drink. I had asked her how much for a palm reading.

'Ten dollars per hand,' she said.

'Just one,' I said and she shrugged.

Her upturned finger tips dance a little on the back of my hand as she talks. She says I have a lot of love to give but don't find love easily. She says I'm a good man. Says I have a kind heart. Then she asks me if I agree with this.

I nod, just a little, not sure if I do or not.

She had told me to make two wishes first, before she took my palm. Then she glanced at my hand and said my wishes were for money and love. But what else in life was there was to wish for?

She says I will own my own business. Good fortune will come my way. I should pursue my dream, she says.

And I'm wondering if she's Hispanic or from the Mediterranean. I wonder how long she's been doing this. Wonder if she treats it like working on a production line. Another palm, another fortune telling.

She says I will come into money and good fortune, but that I must believe in it. But she doesn't tell me that I must believe in love.

Then she holds out her palm for her ten dollars. I glance at it, wondering what I might read there. Like I wonder if she promises everybody romance, money and prosperity. The American dream!

The book stores here are full of books on wealth and love. It's the same on TV. Whole channels devoted to business success or lonely hearts.

The first thing that Madam Sylvia had said was that I don't sleep well. That I wake up feeling drained. She said I have troubled dreams.

My American dreams.

***

In the hotel room there is a sleep CD for playing in the bedside console. A soothing male voice says, 'Lie down. Dim the lights. Remember to breathe one-two-three. Breathe one-two-three. Now tighten the muscles in your neck. Then relax. Tighten and relax.' He runs right down my body, asking me to tighten and relax – but I grow bored with him before he even gets halfway, and I pick up the TV remote control and go around the channel, searching for an anime soft porn channel that might have a young girl who stares at me with big, big eyes, who looks like Rose.

***

I go outside during the trade show and watch the crowds walk past. Security guards and police stand around each public building and monument. Guarding them from terrorists, I guess. Who else would attack freedom? I watch the rich and the poor and the black and the white and the old and young going past me. The police and the professionals, the beggars and tourists. I follow some of them with my gaze, watching long legs or wide arses, or tatty shoes or dark beanies, or just the way one person walks. I watch them disappear into the subways or the buses or a cab or just walk out of sight. So many people. So many lives and dreams. All going somewhere. And none of them is her.

***

Madam Sylvia says my path to success has been blocked by bad luck. She says she can take it away by burning special candles. Nine candles will do it, she says. Ten dollars per candle. And I wonder who will get the most fortune out of that?

I tell her I can afford maybe one candle.

She nods.

I nod. And I'm waiting for her to tell me if things are going to work out with Rose. I'm waiting for her to tell me if we'll ever have children together. Sitting there on an iron garden chair on a Philadelphia sidewalk, unable to ask her what I most want to know.

***

The cab driver I have on my second night in the city says that he's from Nigeria when I ask him about his accent. 'Have you met Nigerians?' he asks.

'Oh yes,' I say. But I leave it at that.

His first turn is a wrong one, taking us down a dark street that's a dead end.

'How long have you been in America?' I ask him.

'A long time now,' he says.

But I'm sure he's lying. I imagine it's the type of answer that he pictures himself saying honestly one day.

I sit forward and look through the gap in the perspex barrier to get a better look at his face as he talks, and he suddenly starts gesticulating wildly, forcing me to jerk my head back a little. He's talking rapidly, about international music and how he has trouble getting the music he likes in America. We talk a little about African music and then I ask him why we're going around the west side of the city, because it's the long way.

'Oh no,' he says. 'There are road works the other way.'

'But I went that way earlier,' I say.

And then he goes quiet. He turns the cab eastwards and cuts through the city centre. By the time we reach my hotel he has driven up forty dollars on the meter. It had only been a ten-dollar ride from my hotel to the function centre.

I slowly count out forty dollars, looking at each note carefully. They're all emblazoned with icons of TRUST and LIBERTY. Still things people are willing to fight for, it seems.

'Don't you have any tip for me?' he asks.

'Sure,' I say. 'Here's a tip. Don't try and cheat people who know where they're going.' Though I know I don't really know.

***

There was this US army ranger sitting by himself in the airport terminal when I arrived. He had on a full desert storm uniform with sand-coloured boots and ranger tabs on his shoulders. All the chairs in the terminal were taken except those about him. As if just the possibility of death was contagious. He had this little techno-box on the seat next to him, plugged into the power point at his feet. He had an earphone and was fiddling with some dials. He smiled every now and then as he worked the techno-box, and most of the people in the terminal were keeping a casual eye on him. Probably thinking of Iraq. Probably thinking of the number of marines and rangers who have died there. Probably wondering where he was flying to. Wondering what he was monitoring on the techno-box.

But no one sat close enough to him to see the screen. To see the Disney characters he was watching on his portable DVD player there.

Fantasy Land, the happiest kingdom of them all!

***

The young lady in the sex shop on fashionable South Street says that every day is a festival day on South Street, but she doesn't know anything about the Independence Day street festival. I dig out the brochure and show her. She reads it carefully and calls for Gloria, who guards the key to the whips cabinet. She's about twenty-five too. All the staff are fairly young things, dressed in black, like you'd expect to see in a independent music store.

The whole place looks like a fashion shop, with cute pink plastic sperms swimming from the ceiling, and U2 playing softly on the in-store speakers, set low on the slate tile floor.

Most of the shoppers are as young as the staff.

'Do you want the pink or the orange one, honey?' they ask each other.

Gloria, who knows all the specifications of the many vibrators, and how to get the best out of each one, doesn't know anything about the street festival either. She gives me a suspicious look and asks where I got the brochure from, as she might scrutinise someone who has given her a dodgy credit card.

Love and money, I think.

***

Down by the waterfront I find there is an Irish-American festival on. It's crowded. So much Irish blood here, flowing along the banks of the Delaware River. New Jersey on the far side, Pennsylvania on this side. This is Penn's Landing, where the American dream was made real. Where liberty was declared. Where America was created.

Tens of thousands of Irish people sailed up the river here and landed at this exact place, carrying little except their dreams – hoping that one day their children, or their children's children, might be able to live and celebrate just like this.

A band is set up, playing Irish pop, and all the small kids are dancing. Mums and dads are sitting on the steps about them, clapping in time to the music, smiling. Guinness T-shirts and Irish flags and Celtic tattoos on arms and calves. I watch the couples who have an arm around each other. Watch them watching their children. Seeing all the happiness there. Such a tribal nation, I think. So fiercely protective of their own. And so willing to consider those who are different as less their own.

And there's a jar-head with a T-shirt that says 'Irish Marine', dancing with his young daughter. They're doing a mix of Riverdance and some jig, and laughing and laughing. And I wonder if one day, years from now, regardless of whatever happens to her dad, she'll remember this. Will dream of it.

***

Walking down the street once I'd left Madam Sylvia's all the things I never asked her crowded into my head. Like if I'd just asked the right questions, she'd have given me a better fortune reading. Where would I be ten years from now? Still flying off to trade shows and still missing Rose? Still fighting when we were together? What dreams might I have for a better life for any children we might have?

And what dreams might trouble me then?

***

It takes me thirty minutes of dialling before I finally get a dial tone on her phone. I'm angrily stabbing the hotel phone buttons over and over in the same pattern, cursing the lines, cursing the operator who tells me I am unable to be connected at this time. Just one more try, I say. Just one. The last one. Okay, one more. And finally it rings. I've worked out the time difference on the hotel note pad, written it down to make sure I've gotten it right. It should be eight in the morning there.

I'm already talking to her in my mind. Telling her I miss her. Telling her about America. Telling her everything. But the phone goes through to her voice mail. Again!

I know why Russell Crowe threw the phone at that hotel guy. If one came to my door now I'd throw this phone at him too.

I hang up and sit there at the hotel desk for some moments. I want to tell her how angry I am. Want to ask her why she never picks up the phone. Want to know where she is when I'm thinking of her.

***

I dream of us that night. It's a dream that changes and morphs. We're in bed together making love. Then it becomes the hotel bed. Then it becomes an anime girl from the hotel adult channel who looks like her in a way Walt Disney never imagined. She gazes out at me and fills me with lust and longing deep in the night as she invites me to press myself against her. Offers to be my guide through my troubled dreams. Her body, as soft as pure white pillows.

***

'You fuckin' bitch!' she screams at me. Screams at the whole world. 'You bitch!' This black woman is walking down the street at night, shouting at the top of her voice, 'You fuckin' bitch! You pussy! I'm going to show you. You BITCH!'

As she gets closer to me, I cross over the road to the other side, where there's this black guy saying, 'That's it, just keep talking that crazy shit!' And I smile to him and he smiles back.

We watch the old lady continue down the street and then he says to me, 'How you doin'?'

And I say, 'Yeah, not too bad.'

And he says, 'Where you from?'

And I tell him.

And then he says, 'Hey, man, you lookin for a bit of cum-fort? I show you this place that can do you a massssage like you've never had before.'

I thank him and say, 'No, I'm not interested.'

'Then can you spare me a couple of dollars for a sandwich?'

'How much?'

'Three – maybe four dollars.'

'That's a lot for a sandwich.'

'Yeah. Sandwiches are expensive downtown,' he says.

Such simple dreams of love and money, I think.

***

Marcus, who I've met at the trade show, is explaining how the American class system works. 'In the north,' he says, 'they need to ask you what school you went to. But in the south they need to ask what family you're from.'

He doesn't tell me what people ask the poor crazy people on the streets. 'What are you angry at?' 'Who are you shouting at?'

The trade show days are long and everybody's out to do business. Out to cut a deal. Out to make money. They're hungry for it. They all float around on this big bubble of expectation of making it big.

I walk around amongst the booths and videos and high-tech

spruikers, not really interested, wishing there was somebody there selling real happiness.

A lot of US states have their own booths at the trade show. The Louisiana booth is handing out bright Mardi Gras bead necklaces, and programs for all the trade shows that will be held at the New Orleans Convention Centre in the next year.

'N'orlens,' they pronounce it. 'Y'all don't want to go home without a visit to N'orlens,' they say.

I take one of the programs, not knowing none of the shows will ever happen.

***

I dream of flying. I dream of travelling the ocean. I dream of taking her away to a new land, far from the troubles that divide us. Where our children might grow up prosperous and happy, and on some sunny Sundays will dance with each other to the bitter-sweet music of their ancestors.

***

Everyone at the trade show is talking about bio-terrorism. All the newspapers and TV news have the story that three mice infected with bubonic plague have gone missing from a local research laboratory. The mice were genetically engineered to carry the plague, everyone says. The infected mice could be released around Philadelphia and infect tens of thousands of people, everyone says. Police and the FBI are on high alert.

There are police everywhere. Sirens scream outside on the streets. Hundreds of people push their way into the convention centre lobby, flooding it with an air of panic and terror. But only the well-dressed and well-off. The poor and the crazies keep walking the streets, as if this is no more terrible than their normal lives.

Everyone at the trade show is tense. Is selling more furiously. Like having money will keep you safe from anything.

It is not until late in the day that the news is passed around that the missing mice were found to have been eaten by other mice in the laboratory. Fed upon by their own. Or is it because they were somewhat less than their own?

'Who'd have imagined that?' people say all about me.

***

I'm wide awake at four a.m., sitting up in bed in my hotel room, flipping through the TV channels, watching bits of movies, and talk shows and early morning evangelists. CNN has the latest US deaths in Iraq. Kevin Kline is impersonating the president of the USA in *Dave*, and is falling for Sigourney Weaver. Will Smith is having a fight with the girl he's after in *Hitch*, and pretending it doesn't hurt like hell inside. Clint Eastwood is leading the marines up a hill that they're going to take from the enemy. 'Praise the Lord,' says one of the TV evangelists, and there's an ad for a get-rich-quick scheme. Then another offering phone-ins to have your love horoscope told. They're all variations of Madam Sylvia, I think. After a while, I start believing that if I keep watching this montage of images it is going to make some sort of sense to me. Maybe.

The call costs for these phone-in ads are exorbitant! And then I find an Asian anime channel, and I wonder what she's doing now? I try and calculate what time it is there. I wish I could find a TV channel that shows me her right now. A channel that bridged the time difference and the hurt. I wish I could find a movie that showed me how things between us might turn out. I'd pay exorbitant call costs for that.

***

I remember the rows of tiny skeletons. I stood in front of the cabinet in the museum, thinking that each one was a foetus. Someone's child. Someone has removed the bones from the bodies and reassembled them to make these tiny skeletons. As thin as cat bones. It made me shiver. Made me feel sick. I remember two small babies who had been cut open so you could see their insides.

I remember the skeletons of the malformed children. Those born with no brain. The co-joined twins that shared the same head. And some people had brought their own children to the museum to see them. That was more upsetting to me than most of the exhibits. These are the things you have bad dreams of. Not things that you expect to see.

Perhaps I'll dream of finding myself in a cabinet like this, one night, chest cut open for everyone to walk past and peer into. I walk around the glass cabinets until I find the exhibit I'd come looking for. The skeletal remains of two bodies, joined at the heart.

I'd though it might help me understand something, but it spooks me terribly. It's like a trade show on death and the different.

***

'Philadelphia is a study in mediocrity,' the taxi driver who takes me back from the medical museum says. 'It's where you end up if you haven't got your shit together enough to reach either Washington or New York.'

'Hell,' he says, 'Even those September 11 hijackers flew right over us without looking down.'

He's the first actual American cab driver I've had and he looks like an ageing hippy. Long grey hair tied back in a ponytail. He tells me that he was born in Philadelphia, but that he has lived most of his life in other places. 'New York. California. Venice beach.' He's followed a bohemian existence all his life, he says, but all the bohemian communities get resettled by six-figure income earners, who dream of the bohemian lifestyle, but kill it by driving all the real free-thinkers out when they send up real estate prices.

'I can't afford to live in any of those places any more,' he says. 'I can only afford to live here in Philly.'

And then he asks me, like everybody does when I tell them where I'm from, 'So how are you enjoying America?'

'It's good,' I say. Then, 'Really good.'

And he asks me if I've been to the art museums and the constitutional museum and Ben Franklin's house, and the Liberty Bell. All those monuments to freedom and liberty around Philadelphia.

'No,' I say.

'Not your idea of America?' he asks.

'Not really,' I say. But what I mean is, I love the idea of America, but I want to know when you lost it.

And then he says, 'It's all on the surface. Scratch the American dream and you find the American nightmare.'

I don't know what to say to that, and he says, 'That's why we don't scratch.'

***

There's a tall black woman at the airport, with a clipboard, directing passengers. The place is crowded. Flights are delayed all over because of some storm in the Gulf. New Orleans is on a hurricane alert, they say. People are fleeing north or looking to change their flights or who knows what. That tension you get around airports is heightened today. Like people can feel something really bad is coming, but nobody knows where it is coming from. Nobody knows just how bad it might be.

I ask her where my plane will be leaving from and she shows me a map. Then she turns the clipboard over. It shows she's a volunteer, offering guidance in return for donations for homeless people. I should have guessed, as she doesn't have a gun. I give her all my coins, which is only a couple of dollars worth, and she puts a hand on my shoulder and says, 'God bless you.'

'Show me once more where I should go,' I ask her. 'I don't want to get it wrong.'

She patiently explains it to me once more. I follow her long thin finger on the map and I feel that she really is being my guide in this. Like she is telling my fortune. Telling me how to walk along the pathway, and go around the limos that obstruct the sidewalk, and avoid the wrong doors, and hop onto my plane and fly back home to her.

Like an emigrant of love leaving for a new land. Hoping to settle against the rivers and shores and landings of her body. And everything bad that had happened since I left her might be nothing but a bad dream.

As if flying away from the approaching hurricane and the lonely hotel nights and the climbing Iraq war death count and the obsessive fortune telling and fortune chasing and the propensity to feed upon those less their own, I actually had any idea of just how bad a bad American dream could be. As if.

He stands in front of the mirror…

He stands in front of the mirror and looks into his own eyes, as he might look into the eyes of a stranger. He wonders if his father's eyes were as dark.

His breathing is remarkably even, he notes. That is good. It is important to show the other three that he is not afraid. The younger two are very nervous, he knows, though they are trying not to show it. Particularly his brother. Death is a man's business, and they want to prove they are men too. They've already dressed and prepared. Are waiting for him outside.

He takes his sash and presses it lightly to his lips, then winds it around his waist. He mumbles a short prayer as he does. As he always does. It fills him with a sense of calm. There has been so much crowding his head these last few days. Train timetables. Maintaining secrecy. Police movements. And that vision of the wrecked train. The roar of it spilling off the rails as its sides splinter. The cries and scream of bodies lying askew in the mud.

Blood and steel, he thinks. That's what he needs to show them with. It will be a signal to his people that they will not endure oppression any more. Will not endure the police harassment and the perpetual prejudice of those in power.

He mutters a curse upon those oppressors. Then he takes another deep breath. It has been so difficult to plan for it all. So easy for it to go wrong still.

He dresses quickly, strapping the body armour they have fashioned to his chest. It is heavy with the weight of metal and the power of destruction. He has told the other three that these garments will protect them, not kill them. Will ensure their destiny.

He leans forward and fits a small woollen cap onto his head. He thinks of his sister who has knitted it for him. He is glad she is not here today. She is too headstrong to keep from wanting to join him. He whispers a prayer for her too.

Then he covers his face, leaving only his eyes showing. He imagines how a photograph of himself would look. It would be something his mother would like to have. Something to remember him by. A shot of the four of them. Standing together. Faces hidden, but eyes blazing like bright stars in a winter night's sky.

It's the picture that all the newspapers would run. They wouldn't ignore him this time. They'd know the full force of his words. Would sit up and listen. Words are dead until we give them life with our blood, he thinks.

He takes a final long deep breath and lets it out slowly.

It's time.

He steps out into the other room and looks at his three friends. Steve Hart. Joe Byrne. And his younger brother, Dan Kelly.

'All right, lads,' he says. He can hear the intermittent shots of police surrounding the small hotel in the dark. He clangs his pistol butt onto his metal chest plate. 'Let's send 'em to hell!'

Big Sister

They begin assembling at night, gathering in dark alleyways, called by text messages or quick whispered phone calls. Tall black-clad guards walk down the lines of hopefuls, with guns held at chest height.

They say that the location of the live eviction is only released about one hour beforehand, yet hundreds find their way to the new assembly point each week. The guards carefully frisk everybody, looking for recording devices or weapons or who knows what else, for the tall men never talk, as if they have taken a strict vow of silence, or have had their tongues cut out. The guards then choose people at random and lead them into a doorway, or down a stairwell and along dim corridors, past patches of darkness and then coloured lights, designed to disorient. From this line, more people are chosen at random and led into isolated rooms. Locked in, in total darkness. Not released until afterwards.

They say it's not for the squeamish.

They also say that only forty of the many hundreds who assemble ever get into the House. The others are left to stand in line and clog the entrances in case anybody should ever attempt a rescue.

You have no sense of time when in line, they say. All watches are forbidden. And they say that you are left there so long you never know if you still might be one of the fortunate this week, or if it's already over. The first you know is when the guards are suddenly all gone and the hopefuls around you are muttering a little louder, less hopeful now, shuffling back and forth, or stepping tentatively out of line. Then an air of disappointment sweeps down the alleyway, or corridor, as people realise that they've missed out again.

So they say.

But for those lucky few who do get into the House, they say it's a large dark room, perhaps an old warehouse, or a derelict open office space. There are seats. Cheap metal fold-up ones. You can imagine that they rock a little on the uneven hard ground, and that those who have made it into the House, but still don't know it yet, try and remain as still as possible, not drawing any attention to themselves. Trying not to let their chair click-clack on the ground, as their legs nervously twitch.

Can you imagine it? The smell of rust and damp and sweat and fear about them. And excitement. Of course, excitement.

They say that some people might end up in that large damp room, on their wobbly chair, feeling their hearts pounding in their chests, thinking to themselves that they've made it. They've really made it into the House. But as the time passes, trying to count off the minutes on their pacing pulse, feeling the sweat that's pooling on their spines chilling a little, perhaps they begin to taste a faint disappointment in the air as they realise that it's happened somewhere else.

But for some, the lucky few, they are sitting there in the darkness, lips dry and nerves tight, and then – Snap! Pow! The House lights come on. Blinding! Everybody shields their eyes. They blink and glance through their fingers, trying to see Gretel. The host. El Gretel, the media call her. She's the confirmation. If she's there, they've made it.

And they're thinking, ohmygodohmygodohmygod! It's her. It's really her. And perhaps they might grasp the arm of the person next to them, able to see for the first time if it is a man or a woman. Able to see how old they are. Able to see how much like themselves they might look.

And El Gretel smiles at them all. Says, 'Hello. Welcome to the House.'

Then that famous smile again. As sharp and dangerous as a curved assassin's knife. In another world she might be a game show hostess. A different type of celebrity, playing to a theatre full of people who cheer and catcall to her. But there's no cheering in the House. Talking is forbidden, they say.

El Gretel adjusts her cowl and those in the front row might be able to see her black-nailed fingers more clearly. Might be able to look into those black-kohl-lined eyes and see something of her that's not possible to see on TV.

Most only ever see her as a grainy image on the screen, or perhaps enhanced a little in the tabloid media, and can only imagine what she looks like up close. Others, in select news stations, get tipped off to the broadcast frequency for this week, and will be able to receive a high-quality direct feed to enable them to conduct a live broadcast of the eviction. They might see something more of her. But it's nothing like seeing her there before you.

And it is always seven minutes. Never more and never less.

Those who are in the House can see the dark-robed men who stand behind the cameras, they say, and see the headsets and microphones wired tightly to their heads. They can see how much of El Gretel's actions are scripted and directed. Can see if men are making hand signals to her. Telling her what to say. How to say it.

Or they can see if it is really her who controls everything.

For everyone wants to know more about El Gretel. There are so many different stories about her. They say that she was a war orphan. They say that she is the daughter of a wealthy Middle-Eastern politician. That she is from Iraq. That she is a Saudi. That she is actually from the USA.

Do those seated there before her see something in her eyes that might tell them? Or do they hear something different in her heavily accented voice, as she addresses the lucky forty gathered there before her, and tells them what they will witness tonight. But, of course they already know. Then she steps closer to them, so close they can see if there are any flaws in her skin. Can see the dark hairs of her eyebrows and the curve of her nose. See those thick red lips. See the way her chin juts.

The rest of her body, apart from the occasional glimpse of her hands, is hidden by her black robes. Do they try and imagine the shape of her body beneath as she tells them of the latest list of outrages, atrocities and inhumanities that have been committed? As she tells them that her god has been witness to too much evil to endure it. As she tells them of children who have been made homeless. Mothers who have been widowed. Men who have starved or been beaten. And she is so calm in her delivery. No hint of emotion. No sense of losing control.

El Gretel never loses control.

And then the lights behind her snap on and those lucky few can finally see the housemates. There are five left this week. Eric. Chantel. Ruben. Melanie. And Ivan. We know them all so well. Know them intimately. Each week the tabloid news shows and press are full of their stories. Where they went to school. Where they have worked. The names of their brothers or sisters and parents. We've seen their relatives for weeks too, sending out their vain appeals for mercy.

But that's not how it works, is it? One leaves the House each week. We all know it. They all know it. And those in the House looking at the five housemates, kneeling there on the concrete floor with dark blindfolds on, know it too. Yet, perhaps, in the back of their minds there had been a small seed of doubt. Something that wishes it not to be real. To all be a complex façade, as some insist it is. But that seed is squashed as soon as the lights go on, and they see the housemates' bruises and bloodstains. See the way they tremble.

So they say.

And I imagine that each of the forty fortunate try and guess who it will be tonight. Eric the US corporation engineer? Chantel the French Red Cross nurse? Ruben the Irish truck driver? Melanie the English aid worker? Or Ivan the Ukrainian mercenary?

Those who have gone before them, the other seven of the chosen twelve, will not be named, of course. They have left the House.

The pundits on the talkback shows have been putting their money on Melanie to go this week. They say it's a surprise that she's lasted this long. She's just too much the Euro-brat bureaucrat. Too cold and impersonal when the camera is in on her. And the best odds are on Ivan, even though he's a mercenary. They're usually the first to go, but Ivan has become a bit of a pin-up boy. The young darling of teenagers and bored housewives the world over. A five-million-dollar reward has been raised by his fans for anybody who can rescue him. But perhaps he'll be the last one to go. The one freed. Who can tell?

And El Gretel, who knows the clock is ticking, walks slowly along the row of housemates, touching each on the head and saying their name. 'Eric!' she says, and those in the front row can see he's peed himself.

He's too old for this treatment. He should be playing with his grandchildren in Iowa. The repeated tension has been too much for him. His heart won't stand it much longer, they say.

'Chantel,' hisses El Gretel and she flinches when El Gretel puts her hand on her head, and then whimpers.

Perhaps she's thinking of her teenage children, their faces so much like her own. And just as worn and strained when we see them on the TV news.

'Ruben,' she says.

He always drops his head a little as she touches it. We all know he's had a hard life. Has done many bad things. But it's hard to condemn him now.

'Mel-anee,' she sings, and perhaps seems to hold onto her just that little bit longer.

Is that a sign? Melanie's sister was widely derided for hiring a clairvoyant to find her. But probably only because it was so unsuccessful.

'And Ivan.' She touches the hair on the back of his neck.

Is that a sign too? Or does she do it just to mess with the hundreds of thousands of young women who profess their love for him?

And the forty chosen who sit there, do they have to bite down on their lips so as not to cry out, 'Ruben! Ruben! Ruben!' or 'Mel-anee! Mel-anee!' like those gathered around the broadcasts do?

But now the seven minutes is nearly up and El Gretel steps back into the darkness and lets the camera pan down the faces of the housemates once more. And, surely, those in the room look at each face carefully, as they might look at the numbers on a roulette table, searching for something to reveal itself to them. Which number will the wheel stop at?

Then El Gretel is suddenly there again, stepping back into the light. With the dark pistol in her hand. Perhaps those in the House can say where it came from. Was it handed to her by one of the unseen guards? Did she pull it out of a holster from within her robes? Or is it still as much a mystery as it is for those who analyse the videos in slow motion.

There is a harsh click-clack, and perhaps those seated on the chairs think that one of them has let their seat rock? Maybe they are confused for a moment trying to work out what the sound was? Or perhaps they know it straight away and think to close their eyes. But cannot. Perhaps they tense their whole body as if El Gretel is aiming the pistol at them.

Then she says it. 'It's time to go…'

And I imagine it's like time stands still then. Each rapid heart beat takes forever to pass. A single drop of sweat falling from one of the housemates' brows falls in infinite slowness. El Gretel's eyes stare deeply into the camera. Those eyes. Those eyes. Those eyes. And that smile. Those lips. Those lips. Those lips. Waiting for her to say it.

It's like that moment of teetering beyond a point of balance, waiting for the fall.

'…Ivan!' She says it so quickly. Puts the gun to Ivan's head and squeezes the trigger.

It will be played over and over and over in slow motion later. We'll see the blood spurt out of Ivan's head. See him fall slowly to the ground as commentators analyse the trajectory of the shot and the splatter of Ivan's brain.

But for those in the House, will it happen so quickly that it seems hard to believe? No! Not Ivan! That was a mistake. Everyone loves Ivan. Not him!

And then El Gretel rips the blindfolds off the other four housemates. Eric. Chantel. Ruben. And Melanie. Lets them see Ivan there on the dusty concrete. Lets them know that he's left the House.

And before they can say anything, before they can even look out at those fortunate few sitting there before them, the seven minutes are up, and the lights snap off again.

Perhaps then those lucky few reach out once more for each other's hands. Perhaps this is the moment they are sick. Or perhaps not. They know they will have to wait until their eyes adjust to the darkness before they try and make their way out of the room, out of the building, back to the darkened alleyway. They won't even know if blood has splattered on them until then.

There will be no sign of El Gretel or her guards. Only the hopefuls, still milling around, wondering if it's happened yet. Waiting for one of the fortunate to press into them and say, to their disbelief, 'It was Ivan! It was Ivan!'

And they can always tell those who had really been there in the House. Those lucky few. Because their eyes are so numb. They have actually seen Sister Gretel there before them in her nun's habit, unlike the hundreds of hopefuls who have missed out once again. Yet they no longer seem to consider themselves so lucky.

Or so they say.